T0032312

IN THE ACT

STORYBOOK ND

CURATED BY GINI ALHADEFF

César Aira, *The Famous Magician*

Osamu Dazai, *Early Light*

Helen DeWitt, *The English Understand Wool*

Natalia Ginzburg, *The Road to the City*

Rachel Ingalls, *In the Act*

László Krasznahorkai, *Spadework for a Palace*

Clarice Lispector, *The Woman Who Killed the Fish*

Yoko Tawada, *Three Streets*

IN THE ACT
RACHEL INGALLS

STORYBOOK ND

Copyright © 1987 by Rachel Ingalls

Published by arrangement with the Georges Borchardt Agency and the estate of Rachel Ingalls

Manufactured in the United States of America
First published clothbound by New Directions in 2023

Library of Congress Cataloging-in-Publication Data
Names: Ingalls, Rachel, author.
Title: In the act / Rachel Ingalls.
Description: First edition. | New York : New Directions Publishing, 2023.
Identifiers: LCCN 2023001747 | ISBN 9780811232043 (hardcover) |
ISBN 9780811232050 (ebook)
Subjects: LCGFT: Novellas.
Classification: LCC PS3559.N38 I6 2023 | DDC 813/.54—dc23/eng/20230203
LC record available at https://lccn.loc.gov/2023001747

10 9 8 7 6 5 4 3 2 1

New Directions Books are published for James Laughlin
by New Directions Publishing Corporation
80 Eighth Avenue, NY 10011

IN THE ACT

As long as Helen was attending her adult education classes twice a week, everything worked out fine: Edgar could have a completely quiet house for his work, or his thinking, or whatever it was. But when the lease on the school's building ran out, all the courses would end—the flower arranging, the intermediate French and beginning Italian, the judo, oil painting and transcendental meditation.

She told Edgar well in advance. He nodded. She repeated the information, just in case. He said, "Mm." Over the next two weeks she mentioned the school closure at least three times. And, after she and her classmates had had their farewell party, she told him all about that, adding, "So, I'll be at home next week. And the week after that. And so on."

"Home?" Edgar said. "What about your adult education things?"

She went over the whole history one more time. At last he was listening. He looked straight at her and said, "Oh. That means you'll have to find something else to occupy yourself with on those afternoons."

"I suppose so. I might stay home and paint here."

"I'll be busy up in the lab."

"I could make a kind of studio down in the cellar."

"I'll be working. I need absolute peace and quiet."

"Well, painting isn't very loud."

"Helen," he said, "I'd like to have the house to myself."

She never got angry with him anymore; that is, she'd discovered that it did no good: he'd just look at her coldly as if she were exhibiting distressing habits usually encountered only among the lower species. Raising her voice—when she'd been driven to it—produced the same reaction from him. She'd learned to be argumentative in a fudgy, forgiving drone she'd found effective with the children: enough of that sound and the boredom level rose to a point where people would agree to anything. Edgar had a matching special tone for private quarrels: knowing, didactic, often sarcastic or hectoring. Whenever he used it outside the house, it made him disliked. It was a good voice for winning arguments by making other people hysterical. His hearing seemed to block off when it started.

She said, "If you'd like the house to yourself, you can have it. Maybe you wouldn't mind fixing some supper for us while you're here. That way, I'd have something to look forward to, soon as I get in from walking around the block five thousand times."

"There's no need for that."

"OK, you can take me out. Twice a week. That'll be nice. We could see a lot of new movies in just a month."

"You're being unreasonable."

"Of course I am. I'm a woman," she said. "You've already explained that to me."

"Let's not get into that."

"Why not? If I'm not even allowed to paint downstairs somewhere for two afternoons a week? I never come up to the attic, do I?"

"You're always tapping on the door, asking me if I want a cup of coffee."

"Only that once."

"It was a crucial moment."

"Well, now you've got your thermos bottle and everything, you're all set up there."

"You came up other times."

"That big noise—explosion, whatever it was: of course I did. I was worried. You could burn the house down."

"I think this is time number fourteen for telling you that the experiments are not dangerous."

"Fourteen? I'm sure that must be right. You keep track of things like that so well. Each time I conceived, it was a positive miracle of timing. I can remember you crossing off the days on the calendar."

"You're trying to sidetrack me."

"I'm trying to get you to allow me to stay in my own house."

"I really do need complete freedom to work. It simply isn't the same when somebody else is in the house. Even if you didn't try to interrupt me again."

"The only other time I knocked on the door was when there was all the screaming."

"I told you," Edgar said. "I got the volume too high."

"It sounded like real people."

"It was a tape."

"For heaven's sake, Edgar—where can I go?"

"See some friends? Look around a museum or two. Find another one of those adult education places."

All at once she felt hurt. She didn't want to argue anymore, even if there was a hope of winning. She was ready to walk out and tramp up and down the streets like a child running away. She said, "I'll try," and went into the living room. She walked around the corner, into the alcove where the desk was. She sat down in the plump, floral-patterned chair, put her knees up and curled into a ball. She heard his feet going up the stairs, then up the next flight to the attic. He wouldn't be wondering whether he'd made her miserable. He'd be getting out the keys to unlock the attic door, which he kept locked all the time, and if he was inside, bolted too. He'd be sighing with pleasure at the prospect of getting back to his experiment. Of course he was right: she'd have to find something to do with her time. But just for a few minutes, she'd stay in the flowered chair, with her arm over her eyes.

The next morning, she was angry. He read through his newspaper conscientiously, withdrawing his attention from it for only a few seconds to tell her that she hadn't cut all the segments entirely free in his grapefruit— he'd hit exactly four that were still attached. She knew, he said, how that kind of thing annoyed him.

She read her letters. Her two sons were at boarding school. Edgar approved. She herself would never have suggested sending, or allowing, the boys to go away: in fact, the suggestion had come from them. They had suddenly clamored for the expensive snobberies of the East Coast; they needed, they wanted, they couldn't live without education at the last of the all-male establishments. Helen's attendance at adult education classes dated from the time of their emigration.

Both of the boys had written to her. Usually she was delighted by whatever they had to say. This morning their news seemed to be nothing but boastful accounts of how they had won some sports event or beaten another boy at something, shown him who was who; and so forth. She was probably lucky they were far away. That would have been two more grapefruits she wouldn't be able to get right.

When she passed the letters over to Edgar, he was soberly pleased with the boys' victories. He wasn't too bad as a father. He wasn't actually too bad anyway, except that sometimes he irritated her to distraction. She still couldn't believe he was asking her to get out of the house every Tuesday and Thursday, so he'd have the whole place to himself.

"What's wrong with the coffeepot?" he added.

She snapped back out of her thoughts. "I was wondering about adult education classes," she told him.

"Fine. More of that flower arranging, or maybe a new language."

"Yes, maybe. Who would I talk to in a new language?"

"Well, the teacher. Anybody else who speaks it." He went back to the paper. Soon afterward he took his last sip of coffee, looked around for his briefcase, and left the house for the pathology laboratories where he had his job. They did a lot of work for the police as well as for hospitals and private clinics. His specialty was hemoglobin.

With the dusting and vacuuming she worked off some of her vexation. Then she sat down with a cup of coffee. She phoned about the plumber's bill, the bracelet link that was supposed to be done but still wasn't, the garage. Nothing was ready. She was about to call up her friend, Gina, to complain about life in general, when she had a better idea: she'd go up to the attic.

She had a key. Long before the day when there was the explosion or the one when she'd heard the screams, she had wanted to see inside his laboratory. The loud noise had at first scared her off from the idea of trespassing, and then reinforced her initial desire: to go in and take a look around—make sure everything was all right up there. The screams too, at first frightening, had made her eager to see, to know; for a few moments she had been convinced that there were real people up there. Not that Edgar would be carrying out any experiment that would cause pain to someone, but—she didn't really know what she thought about it all.

The way he locked the door before he came downstairs; the way he locked up as soon as he entered the lab and shut the door behind him, shooting the bolt across: it made her nervous. If there was nothing inside that could harm her, it was an insult to keep her out. On the other hand, if there was something dangerous up there, did she dare go in and find out about it?

The key was one of the extras from the Mexican bowl that had been shoved over to the end of a workbench in the cellar. The bowl was filled with old keys. Helen had looked through the whole collection when they had moved in; she'd assumed that they came from other houses or even from workplaces long vanished. There were about fifty keys, some large, long and rusted, like the sort of thing that might be needed for a garden gate or a toolshed. After the screams, when her frustration and curiosity about the lab had reached a sudden peak, she'd remembered the bowl of keys. Some could be discounted straightaway, but about a dozen were possible.

The one that fitted was an ordinary brass key. She'd unlocked the door, pushed it open slowly, peeked in and locked up again. She hadn't stepped over the threshold. Now, standing in the middle of her living room rug, she wondered why she hadn't gone in and had a thorough look at everything. She seemed to recall that what was in the room had been fairly uninteresting: tables, benches, racks of test tubes, a microscope, a couple of Bunsen burners, two sinks, a bookcase against the wall. Never mind: this time she'd go through the place carefully.

She got the key and started up the stairs, moving fast. She had the door open before there was time to think about it.

The room looked slightly different from when she'd last seen it, and more crowded. There were more bottles, jars and test tubes. Standing racks had been added at the far end, where the empty steamer trunks used to be. She also remembered a rather nice sofa; more a like a *chaise longue*. Edgar had occasionally stayed up in the lab overnight, working while she'd watched the late movie downstairs, or read a detective story. She'd always thought the sofa was too good to leave up in the attic, but Edgar had insisted that he needed it. Now she couldn't see it. But, as she moved forward, she noticed with surprise that a bathtub had been added to the collection of sinks and troughs; it was an old, high-standing type. She couldn't imagine how Edgar had managed to get it in there. He'd have had to hire people. *Out of the van and to the front door*, she was thinking; *up the stairs*. She began to worry about the weight. Even though the house was well built and strong, and most of the heavy equipment stood around the sides, it wasn't a good idea to fill up a place with too many heavy objects. Edgar had undoubtedly gone into the question of beam stress and calculated the risks; he'd have found out all about the subject. Of course, every once in a while, he was wrong.

She looked into the first alcove: empty. She turned into the second, bigger one. There was the sofa. And there was a bundle of something thrown on top of it, wrapped in a sheet. She was about to pass by when she saw a hand protruding from one of the bottom folds of the sheet.

She let out a gurgled little shriek that scared her. She looked away and then back again. Propped against the edge of the sofa's armrest was a leg, from the knee down. Next to it lay an open shoe box containing fingers. She began to feel that her breathing wasn't right. She wanted to get out, but there was still the question of what was under the sheet. She had to know that. If she ran out without looking, she'd never summon the courage to use the key again.

She counted to ten, wiped her hands down the sides of her skirt and told herself that whatever the thing was, it couldn't be worse than what they were liable to show you nowadays on television, even in the news programs. She reached out and pulled down the edge of the sheet.

It was pretty bad: a head with the face laid bare. The muscles, tendons and other bits across the face were mainly red or pink, a few of them darker than she'd imagined things like that were supposed to be. But they weren't wet; there was no blood. She bent her knees and looked more closely. From inside the still open skull she caught the glint of metal. There were lots of small wheels and bolts and tubes inside, like the interior of a watch or a radio.

She straightened up, rearranged the sheet and gently put out a hand toward the half leg. She felt the skin below the place where the joint should have been attached to some knuckly part of a knee.

A chill ran over her scalp. The skin, though unwarmed, was creamy, smooth, soft and silky, uncannily delicious to the touch. She pulled back her hand. For about five minutes she stood just staring at the wall. Then, she understood. The body wasn't real. Naturally, it couldn't be real: a dead body would have to be refrigerated. Therefore, that thing there on the sofa in pieces was not a corpse Edgar had taken from the pathology morgue; it was a body he had built himself out of other materials. Why on earth he'd want to do such a thing was beyond her.

She left everything in place, closed the door behind her and locked it with her key. Later in the day the answer came to her: her husband must be pioneering research on victims of road accidents. She had read an article several years before, about a medical school that simulated injuries by strapping life-sized replicas of people into cars; after smashing them up, they studied the damaged parts. The project had been funded by an insurance company. No doubt Edgar was working on something similar, although greatly in advance of anything she'd heard about. That skin, for example, was fantastic. And all the intricate bands of muscle and everything—the thing was very complicated. She still didn't understand what the clockwork mechanism in the head would be for, but maybe that would have something to do with a remote-control guidance system. The whole business was explainable. She stopped feeling scared. Nevertheless, she was thankful that the eyelids had been closed.

Edgar worked hard up in the attic for several days. She thought she'd give him a week and then go up and check on the progress he'd made. In the meantime, she looked into the possibilities of new adult education schools. She had lunch with Gina, who was worried about her daughter's weight problem and who poured out a long story to her about psychologists, behaviorists, weight-watchers and doctors. Helen listened sympathetically; she was glad to have such a convoluted narrative to concentrate on—there was no room for temptation to talk about what was troubling her: Edgar and the activity he was engaged in up in the attic.

Two days later, Mr. Murdock from the old oil painting classes asked her to tea with Pat and Babs. The three of them cheered her up. Mr. Murdock had already left the new classes they'd joined; the other two were going to, but for the moment they were sticking it out in order to be able to report back all the latest stories about the odious Miss Bindale. Miss Bindale was driving everyone away; she might end by causing the teacher to resign, too. It was a shame, they all said: one person could spoil everything. Mr. Murdock recommended a language school he'd gone to for French. The place wasn't so much fun as their adult education school—it was more serious, the classes were mostly for businessmen and unless you applied for the weekend, everything was in the evening. Pat said, "It'd be a really good way to meet men. If you don't want the address, I'll keep it myself."

"You'll never get anywhere if it's a language," Babs told her. "Car maintenance, that's the one. There aren't any other women at all."

"Or karate," Helen said.

"I wouldn't try it. You pick the wrong type there—they'll throw you against the wall and say it was an accident because they forgot to leave out some basic move. No thanks."

Pat said that a friend of hers, named Shirley, had gone to a couple of other adult education places and had given her the addresses; four different ones. "I liked the first one, so I never tried the others, but I can send you the addresses. I'll take a good look around, see where I put that piece of paper."

Edgar spent the whole of the weekend up in the lab: Saturday night and Sunday too. He came down for meals. On Friday he'd brought her flowers, given her a talk about why the work was going to be necessary; when, where and how he'd expect his meals during the period; and how he appreciated her cooperation. She said, "Yes, dear," to everything, put his red roses in a vase, took it into the living room and told him they looked lovely. She preferred daffodils, chrysanthemums, tulips, daisies, stock, sweet peas, asters: almost anything. And if they had to be roses, any color other than red.

He stayed in the bedroom Friday night, making sure that she didn't feel neglected. He wanted her to be satisfied with the arrangements. She was not only satisfied; she was surprised.

She carried out her appointed cooking tasks with grim cheerfulness. She could hardly wait until Monday, when he'd be out of the house and she could go look at what he'd been doing.

On Sunday she knew that he'd achieved some kind of breakthrough in the work. He was transformed, radiant. He looked tired, but serene. Whatever it was, was finished. However, he didn't say anything about coming downstairs. He stayed up in the attic that night.

The next morning she waited awhile after he'd gone. She was going to give him enough time to get all the way to work, and more: in case he'd forgotten some-thing and had to come back for it. She wanted to be able to look at everything and not feel rushed. Whatever he'd completed was still up in the attic—all he'd taken with him was his briefcase.

She did the dishes, made the bed, checked her watch. She looked out of the window, although she didn't need to: it was one of those unnecessary things people do when they're anxious about something. She got the key.

The attic workroom looked the same, as far as she could see. She stepped in, closing the door lightly, so that it touched the jamb but didn't click into the frame. She walked forward. Her eyes jumped from place to place.

She peered into the first alcove: nothing. She hur-ried to the second; there was the sofa. And on it lay a young and beautiful woman: the creamy skin was as it had been before. The face had been fitted with its outer coating; everything there was in place: the lilac-tinted eyelids with long, dark lashes, the cupid's-bow mouth, the small, pert nose.

The face lay in the center of a cloudlike nest of twirly blond ringlets. A blue ribbon peeped out from a bunch of them at the back. The dress she wore was pink and cut like some sort of ballerina costume: the bodice like a bathing suit top, the skirt standing out with layers of net and lace and stiffening. Her feet and legs were bare. The toenails, like the nails on the fingers, had been painted red.

Helen reached out toward the left leg. She ran her

hand over it, stopped, and then quickly pulled back. The skin was warm. She moved along the side of the sofa, to where she could be near the head. "Wake up," she ordered. There was no response. Naturally: this wasn't a person—it was some kind of doll. It was so lifelike that it was almost impossible to believe that; nevertheless, her husband had built it.

As she stood there, trying to imagine why Edgar should have made a doll so detailed in that particular way, with painted nails and a blue satin bow and everything, she began to wonder how lifelike the rest of the body was. That was an important question.

If she hadn't seen the thing in its partly assembled state the week before, she wouldn't have known this was a replica, a machine. But having seen it complete, there was—all at once—no doubt in her mind that her husband had invented it for his own private purposes: otherwise, why make it so definitely nonutilitarian?

She thought she'd better know what she was up against. She examined the doll thoroughly, taking off the pink dress first, and then the black lace bra and underpants. She started to lose her sense of danger. She was getting mad. Who else, other than Edgar himself, could have chosen the pink dress and black underwear? He couldn't walk into a dress shop in her company without becoming flustered, yet she could picture him standing at a counter somewhere and asking for the clothes, saying in his argument-winning voice, "Black lace, please, with a ribbon right about here." He'd known the right size, too—but of course he'd known that. The doll had been built to specification: his specifications. *Oh*, Helen thought, *the swine.*

And the thing was so real-looking. She was sitting on the edge of the sofa and fiddling around with the doll's head, investigating the way the hair grew, when she felt her finger push down on what must have been a button behind the left ear.

The doll's eyelids rose, revealing a pair of enormous blue eyes. The lips parted in a dazzling smile, the torso began to breathe.

"Oh," Helen said. "Oh dear."

"Oh dear," the doll repeatedly gently. "What can the matter be?"

Helen thought she might be going crazy. She asked—automatically and politely—"Who are you?"

"I'm fine," the doll told her. "How are you?"

"Not how. Who?"

The doll smiled lovingly and relapsed into an expression of joyful delight. The eyelids blinked every once in a while. Helen watched. The action had evidently been programmed to be slightly irregular, to avoid an impression of the mechanical. Still, there was something hypnotic about it. The lips were silent. The voice too must be on a computer: the doll would only answer if you spoke to it. The voice-tape scanner didn't seem to be quite perfect yet, either.

She was trying to push the button again, to turn off the eyelids, when she hit a nearby second button instead and sent the machine into overdrive. The lids drooped, the arms went up and out, the knees flew apart, the hips began to gyrate in an unmistakable manner, and the lips spoke.

Helen shot to her feet, stumbled back a few steps and crashed against the wall. She folded her arms and stayed where she was, staring with memorizing intensity while the doll went through the cycle it had begun. Probably there were many other things it could do—this would be merely one of the variations. Out of the rosebud mouth came a mixture of baby talk and obscenity, of crude slang and sentimentality.

She gripped the sides of her arms and waited sternly until the exercise appeared to be over, though the doll was still begging in sweetly tremulous whispers for more. She stepped forward and slapped it across the face. "Darling," it murmured. She scrabbled among the golden curls, grabbed the ear and pushed every button she could see. There were five, all very small. They looked like pinheads. There were also two tiny switches she decided to leave alone. She'd seen enough. She was quivering with rage, shame and the need for revenge.

When she thought about wearing herself out doing the shopping and cooking and scrubbing, she prickled all over with a sense of grievance. She'd been slaving away for years, just so he could run up to the attic every evening and keep his secrets. And the boys were turning into the same kind as their father: what they wanted too was someone menial to provide services for them. And then they could spend their lives playing.

She saw herself as a lone, victimized woman beleaguered by selfish men. Her anger gave her a courage she wouldn't otherwise have had.

She ran out and across the hall to the other side of the attic—the side that wasn't locked. There were the trunks and suitcases, including the nice big one with wheels. There too was the chest full of spare blankets and quilts. She pulled out two of the blankets and took them into the lab. Then she carried the suitcase downstairs to the front hall.

She went up to the attic again, dressed the doll in its clothes, rolled it into the blankets and dragged them across the floor and down the stairs. She unzipped the suitcase, dumped the doll inside, folded the legs and arms and began to pack it tight, zipping the outside as she stuffed the pink skirt away.

She went up to the attic one more time, to put the blankets back and to shut the door of the lab.

She got her coat and handbag. The suitcase was easy to manage until she had to lift it into the back of the car. That wasn't so easy. Edgar was the one with the big car. Still, she could do it. All she'd have to worry about would be steps. The doll seemed to weigh exactly the same as a real woman of equivalent height and size.

There were three choices: the airport, the bus depot and the train station. The train station was large and nearer than the airport. She'd try it first.

Everything went well. She found a parking space straightaway and was able to wheel the suitcase across the road, onto the sidewalk and through the doors, up an escalator and across several waiting rooms, to the locker halls. There was a whole bank of extra-large lockers; she heaved the case into one of them, put in enough money to release the key, and went to get some more coins. She ended up having to buy a paperback book, but the woman at the cash register agreed to let her have two big handfuls of change. She fed the money meticulously into the slot. The suitcase would be paid up for over two weeks.

Ron was getting out of his car when he saw the woman slam her car door and start to wheel the suitcase across the parking lot. She looked possible: the case seemed heavy.

He followed, walked casually. He had a repertoire of walks calculated to throw off suspicion. He hadn't had to learn any of them—they came naturally, like all his other athletic talents. That was what he was always telling Sid down at the gym: *I got natural talent. I don't need nobody teaching me nothing.* He still couldn't understand how Sid had knocked him out in the third round. He hadn't given up the idea that something had been slipped into his Coke. Sometimes there was a lot of heavy betting going on, even when you were just sparring.

She looked like a nice, respectable woman; pretty, took care of herself. The kind that said no. Her clothes cost something, which was a good sign; so was the trouble she had getting the wheels of the case up onto the curb. Of course, she could be getting on a train.

He followed her all the way around the corner to the

lockers. He watched, standing against the wall and pretending to look at his paper. When she was through, he followed her far enough to see that she was coming back. She put a lot of money in the locker: good—the case would be there a while. But he'd probably better get it quick, before somebody else did.

She left the building. That might mean she was going for a second suitcase that she hadn't been able to handle in the same load. He looked around, folded his paper, held it to cover what he was doing, and stepped up to the locker. He took a metal slide out of his pocket and stuck it into the keyhole. It was a cinch.

Some people could never have looked unsuspicious while wheeling away stolen luggage, but you had to believe in yourself: that was the main thing. Ron did his best. He didn't hurry. He got the bag into the backseat of his car and started off. Her car, he noticed, was already gone.

Normally he'd have stopped just around the block somewhere, to go through the contents; but the traffic was building up. He decided to drive straight on home. He was beginning to get curious about what was inside. The suitcase was really heavy. The moment he'd pulled it from the locker he'd thought: *Great—gold bars; silver candlesticks.* A lot of people had those lockers. She hadn't looked like that type, but how could you ever tell? She could be helping a pal, or a husband. A guy he knew had found some cash once—a whole overnight bag full of the stuff. And all of it counterfeit, it turned out; he'd done time for that.

He got the bag out of the car, into the apartment block where he lived, up three floors in the elevator, down the hall to his bedroom. He broke the locks as soon as he'd thrown his jacket over the back of the easy chair. He unzipped both sides.

A powerful odor of mothballs was released into the room as the lid sprang open, disclosing a blond woman in a pink dress. She was huddled up like a baby rabbit, and he was sure she was dead. He'd be suspected, of course. He'd have to ditch the case someplace, fast. He put his hand on her arm to squash her in again. The arm was warm. He jumped away. He closed the curtains and turned on the lights.

He couldn't put her back. She might be alive now, but soon she'd suffocate. It was a good thing he'd found her in time. When he thought of that respectable type who'd shut her in the locker, he was amazed.

He got the plastic sheet he'd used to cover his Norton Atlas before one of his friends had borrowed the machine and smashed it to pieces. He spread the sheet over the bed and lifted the woman on top of it. He thought she looked fabulous, just like a dream. She seemed to be unharmed except for a mild discoloration on her left cheek, which might have been sustained in the packing. There was no blood that he could see. He thought he'd better do a complete check, to make sure she was all right. He took off her clothes. The dress was a bit weird, but she had some pretty classy underwear. Under the underwear was OK, too. He thought he might have some fun with her, while he was at it. He'd saved her life, after all: she owed him.

He was beginning to wonder what was going on—despite the warmth, she didn't actually seem to be breathing—when, accidentally, as he was running his hand through her hair, the side of his thumb hit two tiny, hard knobs of some kind and his problems were over.

The woman sighed and stretched out her arms. Her hands came softly around his back. Her eyes opened, her mouth smiled. She said, "Ooh, you're so nice."

Helen was curled up in her favorite living room chair when Edgar came in from work. She was reading the paperback she'd had to buy at the station; a nurse novel called *Summer of Passion*. She heard the car, the slam of the door, his feet crunching on the gravel of the driveway, the door being opened and shut. He called out, "Hi," going up the stairs. She answered, and read to the end of the paragraph: *at last Tracy knew that she had found the man of her desires and that this summer of passion would live in her heart forever.* Helen yawned. She put the phone bill between the pages of the book and stood up. Edgar was taking his time. Maybe he was running around the attic in circles, every time coming back to the empty sofa and not believing it. She didn't feel sorry. She felt mean-hearted, even cruel, and absolutely satisfied. Let him be on the receiving end of things for a while. It might do him some good.

The attic door slammed. He'd figured out she had

to be the one to blame. He came thundering down the stairs and across the front hall. She put the book down on the coffee table. Edgar dashed into the room, breathing loudly. His hair was sticking up, as if he'd been running his hands through it. "Where is she?" he demanded.

"Who?"

"My experiment. You know what I'm talking about."

"Oh? It's a she, is it?"

"Where is she?" he shouted. "You get her back here, or you're going to wish you'd never been born." He took a step forward.

"Oh, no, you don't," she said. "You lay a finger on me, and you'll never see her again."

"What have you done with her?"

"That's my business. If you want her back, we're going to have to talk it over."

He looked defiant, but he gave in. She took up her stance by the red roses, he struck a pose in front of the Chinese lamp with the decorations that spelled out Good Fortune and Long Life. He said, "You don't know what you've done. It's a masterpiece. It's as if you'd stolen the Mona Lisa. The eyes—my God, how I worked to get the eyes right. It's a miracle."

A woman, she thought, *can get the eyes and everything else right without any trouble: her creative power is inherent. Men can never create; they only copy. That's why they're always so jealous.*

"What's her name, by the way?" she asked.

He looked embarrassed, finally. "Dolly," he said.

"Brilliant. I suppose you're going to tell me this is love."

"Helen, in case you still haven't grasped it after all these years—my main interest in life is science. Progress. Going forward into the future."

"OK. You must let me know how long it's going to take you to come up with the companion piece."

"What?"

This was her moment. She thought she might begin to rise from the floor with the rush of excitement, the wonderful elation: dizzying, intoxicating, triumphant. This was power. There was even a phrase for it: drunk with power. No wonder people wouldn't give it up once they got hold of it. It was as if she'd been grabbed by something out of the sky, and pulled up; she was going higher and higher. Nothing could hurt her. She was invulnerable.

"I want," she said, "what you had—something nice on the side. A male escort: presentable, amusing, and a real stud."

"No way."

"Then I guess it's goodbye, Dolly."

"If you don't tell me—"

"Don't you dare touch me," she shrieked. "It's all right for you to play around in my own home, while I'm down here doing the housework, isn't it?"

"I don't think you understand."

"I don't?"

"It's just a doll."

"Pubic hair and nipples everywhere you look—that's

some doll. And what about that twitch and switch business she does? That's a couple of giant steps ahead of the ones that just wet their pants and cry mama."

"It may turn out to have important medical uses. Ah ... therapeutic."

"Good. That's just what I'm in need of."

"Helen," he said, "let's forget all about this."

"OK. It isn't that important to me. I can find a real man anywhere. But if you want your Dolly back, you can make me a perfect one. That's only fair. One for you and one for me."

"I don't know why you're so steamed up."

"I'm not that crazy about adultery, that's all. Especially if I'm the one who's being acted against."

"There's no question of adultery. In any case—well, in any case there's no moral lapse unless it's done with another person."

"No kidding? I thought the moral lapse was there even if you only did it in the mind."

"Let me explain it to you."

"Fine," she told him. "Just as long as you keep working at my gigolo. And if there aren't any lapses, we're both in the clear, aren't we?"

The instant Dolly opened her eyes, Ron fell in love with her. Everything was different. Everything was solved. He'd never thought it would happen to him. He hadn't believed in it: Love. It was going to come as a big surprise to his friends down at the gym—they'd all agreed long ago that life was a lot better without women. They'd just have to get used to her. She was part of his life now. The fact that she was a doll he regarded as an advantage. You didn't need to feed her or buy her drinks or stop the car so she could keep looking for a rest room every five minutes. She was unchanging. The extraordinary skin she possessed cleaned and preserved itself without trouble; the mark on her cheek faded even before the smell of mothballs had worn off. A fresh, springlike fragrance seemed to breathe from her body. His friends would have to accept her as they'd have had to if he'd gotten married. That was what things were going to be like—like having a wife, except that not being human, of course, she was nicer.

That first day, he figured out how to use all the push buttons. He knew her name because she told him: she got right up close to his face, winked, gave a little giggle and whispered, "Dolly wants to play." She was so good at answering his questions that it took him some time to realize she was repeating, and that if he asked a particular question, she'd always give the same response, or one of several set replies. A similar repetitiveness characterized some of her physical reactions, but he didn't mind that. And when you thought about it, her conversation wasn't much more limited than most women's. She sometimes said something that didn't fit, that was all—never anything really stupid. And if she came up with the wrong wording, that wasn't her fault. It almost never happened. Her answers were so good and she was so understanding about everything, that he believed she knew what he was getting at; even if she was a doll, even if she wasn't real in any way. To him she was real. When he looked into her beautiful eyes, he was convinced that she loved him. He was happy. He was also sure that there were no others like her. There could be only one Dolly.

He told her everything. All about himself, what he wanted out of life, what his dreams of success used to be, how he'd grown up: all the things he used to think. He didn't know what he thought anymore and he didn't have any dreams left. He cried in her arms. She stroked his hair and called him darling. She said, "Hush, darling. It's all right." He believed her. He talked to her for hours. He knew that if she could, she'd speak as freely as he did.

Edgar applied for emergency leave from his job. It knocked out the holiday they'd been planning to take with the boys in the summer vacation, but he needed the time. He worked all day and most of the night. Helen brought up his meals on a tray. She tried to make comments once. He screamed at her. He shouted threats, oaths and accusations, ending up with a warning that if she didn't shut up about absolutely everything, he wouldn't be responsible. She smiled. She said in her gooey, peacemaker's voice, "What a pompous twerp you've turned into, Edgar." It was all out in the open now.

And he no longer felt guilty about his infidelities, mental or physical. It served her right. He wished that he'd been more adventurous, all the way back to the beginning, when they'd married: he wished he'd led a double life—a triple one. It was galling to be so hard at work, wasting the strength of his body and brain on the creation of a thing intended to give her pleasure. He could do it, of course; he had mastered the technique and the principles. But it was infuriating. It seemed to him now that there hadn't been a single moment when she'd been anything but a hindrance to him. She nagged, she had terrible moods, she wasn't such a wonderful cook, every once in a while she made a truly embarrassing scene—like the one at Christmas with his uncle—and she could wear really dumpy clothes that he didn't like. She'd keep wearing them after he'd expressly told her he didn't like them. And he didn't think she'd brought the boys up that well, either. They got away from her just in time.

He had needed Dolly in order to keep on living with his wife. If he couldn't have Dolly back, there was no point in going on. Now that there was no longer any secrecy, there was probably no more hope for his marriage. Still, as long as he could recover Dolly, there was hope for him.

When he thought about Dolly, he was ready to go through any trial, do any amount of work. He missed her. He missed the laugh in her voice and the look in her eyes when she said, "Let's have a good time. Let's have a ball."

He lost his concentration for a moment. The scalpel slipped. The voice box let out a horrible cry. He waited to see if Helen would come charging up the stairs to crouch by the banisters and listen. Nothing happened.

Now that she knew, she wasn't worried. She'd wait and be silent.

At the beginning Ron was satisfied with keeping Dolly in his bedroom. But as he began to depend on her, he felt the desire to take her out. He'd found the buttons to make her walk and respond to his request for her to sit down or get up. A mild pressure on her arm would help her to change pace, turn a corner. Naturally the pink dress wasn't right for outdoor wear. He bought her a T-shirt and a skirt. She looked great in them. But the shoes were a problem: you had to try them on. He didn't want to spend money on the wrong size. He asked his friend Charlie, in a general way, what to do if you didn't know your size and couldn't put the shoes on to find out: if you were buying a present, say. Charlie told him to try L. L. Bean. "All you need to do," he told Ron, "is send them a tracing of your foot."

He had a lot of fun making the tracings with Dolly. He sent away for a pair of flat shoes. When they arrived, he walked her around the room in them for a long time, examining the skin on her feet at intervals. He didn't know what would happen if her skin got badly broken or damaged. He had no idea where he could take her to be fixed. He asked if the shoes felt OK; she said everything was just fine and she loved him—he was wonderful.

He sent away for a pair of high heels and some rubber boots as well as socks, a parka, a shirt and a sweater, a pair of corduroy trousers and a blue and white flannel nightgown with ruffles around the neck. He also went out and bought some fingernail polish. Her nails appeared to be indestructible, but the polish was chipping. The girl behind the counter gave him a little lecture about the necessity of removing the old polish before putting on a second coat. She sold him quite a lot of cosmetic equipment. He thought, since he was there, he might buy eye makeup and lipstick, too. "Does it come with instructions?" he asked. The salesgirl sold him a book with pictures and an expensive box full of tiny brushes.

He got hold of of an airport case that contained a roll of traveler's checks and five silk suits. He won on the races and after that, at the tables. Dolly was bringing him luck.

He took her out. People turned to look at her because she was so beautiful, not because they thought something was wrong. He felt like a million dollars walking down the street with her. It was too bad that he couldn't get her to eat or drink, because then he'd be able to take her into a restaurant or a bar. But just walking along, arm in arm, was nice. One afternoon he bumped into Charlie, who took a look at Dolly and nearly fell over. "Jeez, Ron," he said, "what a doll."

Dolly wrinkled up her nose and giggled. She squirmed a little with excitement. Her eyes got bigger.

"Jeez," Charlie said again. "You going to introduce me?"

"Charlie, this is Dolly," Ron said. "Say hi, honey."

"Hi, honey," Dolly said. She put her hand in Charlie's.

Charlie said, "Oh boy. You been holding out on us,

pal. Hi there, Dolly. I don't know why my old buddy Ron here didn't tell me about you before."

"We got to be going," Ron said.

"Oh, come on. You don't have to go, do you, Dolly?"

"Yes," Ron said. "Say goodbye, sugar pie."

Dolly twiddled her fingers at Charlie. She gave him a breathy, hiccuping laugh and then whispered, "Goodbye, sugar pie."

"Oh boy," Charlie said again.

Ron pulled her away fast. She clip-clopped beside him quickly in her high heels, her hips swaying, her large eyes roving happily.

It hadn't gone too badly, but he didn't trust her for extended conversation. He figured they'd better put in some practice first.

He took on a job delivering goods for a friend. Everything was packed up in boxes. Maybe the boxes contained stuff he shouldn't know about. Normally he wouldn't care, but now he kept thinking about Dolly: what would happen to her if he got caught? She'd be found by somebody else, who'd take her away and keep her, just the way he had.

He stopped checking out the airport lockers. He began to look through the papers for legitimate work. Down at the gym they thought he was crazy—at least, they did at first. Word had gone around about Dolly; everybody asked about her. When was Ron going to bring her in to meet the gang?

He coached her for a while and then took her down to the gym. They all loved her. And they thought she was real. They said they could understand how Ron would want to settle down to something steady, if he had a girl like that. An older man named Bud actually clapped him on the shoulder and said something about wedding bells.

Ron wondered if maybe he could get away with introducing her to his sister and her family. He didn't see why not. He phoned Kathleen. She said sure.

"Only thing is," he explained, "she's on this very strict diet, so she won't eat anything. I thought I'd better tell you."

"Well, I can fix her a salad."

"No, it's sort of everything. She's allergic."

Kathleen told him not to worry. He put Dolly into the car, together with a change of clothes and her rubber boots. He drove carefully, thinking all the time that if they crashed, or if she were to cut herself in some other way, he wouldn't know what to do, where to take her. He didn't even know what was inside her; if she got hurt seriously, whatever was in there might all leak out.

Kathleen decided, as soon as she saw Dolly: she didn't like her. Her husband, Ben, thought Dolly was great. The children liked her too, but they didn't understand why she wouldn't pat their dog, when it was evidently so interested in her and kept sniffing around her. Ron grabbed the dog and kept it by him. Later in the afternoon while they were walking along the path by the creek, the dog ran ahead and almost made Dolly trip over. At that moment Ron thought it couldn't work: his friends at the gym were going to accept her, real or not, but his family never would.

Before he drove off he sat Dolly in the car, walked back to where Kathleen was standing, and asked, "Well? Do you like her?"

"Sure. She's fine," Kathleen said. "A little dumb, maybe."

"But nice. She's got a heart of gold."

"I guess it's just—if people are really silly all the time, it's too much like being with the kids. I start to get aggravated."

All the way back to town he felt angry. It wasn't right that he should have to hide Dolly away like a secret vice. She should be seen and admired.

The next day he took her on an expedition into town: through the parks, into the big stores, around one of the museums. The weather was good, which was lucky. He didn't know how she'd react to rain or whether she'd be steady on her feet over wet sidewalks. Of course, he didn't know how a prolonged exposure to sunlight was going to affect her, either, but she seemed all right. Her feet, too, looked all right.

He took her by public transport, since that was part of the idea. They rode on the subway, then they changed to a bus. He had his arms around her as usual, when one of the other passengers got up from the seat behind them, knocking Ron's arm and the back of Dolly's head as he went by. Ron clutched her more tightly; inadvertently he hit several of the control buttons.

Dolly's arms raised themselves above her head, her eyelids flickered, her legs shot apart, her hips began to swing forward and back. "Ooh," she said, "you're so good."

He tried to find the switch. He panicked and turned it on higher by mistake.

She went faster, gasping, "Oooh, you feel so nice, ooh do it to me."

He fumbled at her hairline while people around them said, "Come on, mister, give us a break," and "That's some girlfriend you've got—can't you do it at home?"

He found the switch just as she was telling him—and the whole bus—the thing she loved best about him.

The driver put on the brakes and said, "OK, Mac, get that tramp out of my bus."

Ron refused. If he got out with Dolly before he'd planned to, he'd never be able to walk her to where they could get a cab or find another bus. "She can't help it," he said. "She's sick."

The driver came back to insist; he had a big beer belly. Ron got ready to punch him right in the middle of it and then drive the bus away himself. Dolly slumped against him, her face by his collarbone, her eyes closed. "It just comes over her sometimes," he said. That wasn't enough of an explanation, apparently. He added, "She had a real bad time when she was a kid."

The bus went quiet. Everyone thought over the implications of what Ron had said. The driver went back to the wheel. The bus started up again. Still no one spoke. The silence was beginning to be painful. Ron didn't know why he'd chosen that particular thing to say, even though it had worked—it had shut everybody up fine. But it left him feeling almost as strange as everyone else seemed to. By the end of the ride he'd begun to have a clear idea of the appalling childhood Dolly must have lived through. And he promised himself to take even better care of her than before, in order to make up for her sad life.

When his stop came, he carried her out in his arms. She appeared to be asleep. A few of the other passengers made hushed exclamations and murmurs of interest as he left.

He had to admit that there was always going to be a risk if he took her out in public. Driving alone with her in the car wouldn't be such a problem. He wanted to take her to the beach; to camp in the dunes and make love on the sands at night. He thought her skin would be proof against the abrasions of sand, the burning of the sun, the action of salt water. But he wasn't sure. The more he thought about her possible fragility, the more he worried. If he were hurt, even severely, he could be put together again: but could she?

Helen did the shopping, cooked the meals and began a thorough cleaning of everything in the house: the curtains, the chair covers, the rugs. She wouldn't have a spare moment to use for thought. She wanted to maintain her sense of outrage at a high level, where it could help to keep her active. She had no intention of breaking down into misery. She vacuumed and ironed and dusted. She washed and scrubbed. Once, just for a moment, her anger subsided and she felt wounded.

Edgar had done all that, she thought—he'd been driven to it—because she wasn't enough for him. She obviously hadn't been good enough in bed, either, otherwise he wouldn't have needed such a blatant type as compensation for her deficiencies. Her only success had been the children. She should really give up.

She caught herself just in time. She thought hard against despair, whipping her indignation up again. If things were bad, you should never crumple. Do something about it—no matter what. She stoked her fury until she thought she could do anything, even break up her marriage, if she had to. She was too mad to care whether she wrecked her home or not. *Let him suffer for a change*, she thought.

She could sue him: win a divorce case hands down. You could cite anybody nowadays. There had been a story in the papers recently about a man whose wife, without his knowledge, and—if he'd known—against his will, had had herself impregnated by a machine in a sperm-bank clinic. The husband had accused as corespondent, and therefore father of the child, the technician who'd switched on the apparatus. The fact that the operator of the machine was a woman had made no difference in law. And soon you'd be able to say it was the machine itself. Helen could name this Dolly as the other woman. Why not? When she produced the doll in court and switched on the buttons that sent her into her act, they'd hand the betrayed wife everything on a plate: house, children, her car, his car, the bank accounts—it would be a long list. If she thought about it, she might rather have just him. So, she wasn't going to think about it too hard. She kept on doing the housework.

Up in the attic Edgar worked quickly—frenetically, in fact—although to him it seemed slow. When the replica was ready, he brought it downstairs to the living room and sat it on a chair. He called out, "Helen," as she was coming around the corner from the hall. She'd heard him on the stairs.

"Well, it's ready," he told her.

She looked past him at the male doll sitting in the armchair. Edgar had dressed it in one of his suits.

"Oh, honestly, Edgar," she said.

"What?" He sounded close to collapse. He probably hadn't slept for days.

She said, "He looks like a floorwalker."

"There's nothing wrong with him. It's astounding, given the short time—"

"He looks so namby-pamby. I bet you didn't even put any hair on his chest."

"As a matter of fact—"

"You didn't?"

"The hair is extremely difficult to do, you know. I wasn't aware that all women found it such a necessary item. I understand a lot of them hold just the opposite view."

"And the skin. It's too smooth and soft-looking. It's like a woman's."

"Well, that's the kind I can make. Damn it, it's an exceptionally lifelike specimen. It ought to give complete satisfaction."

"It better," she said. She glared at the doll. She didn't like him at all. She moved forward to examine him more closely.

"And now," Edgar announced, "I want Dolly."

"Not till I've tried him out. What's this? The eyes, Edgar."

"They're perfect. What's wrong with them?"

"They're blue. I wanted them brown."

"Blue is the color I know how to do."

"And he's so pale. He almost looks unhealthy."

"I thought of building him so he'd strangle you in bed."

She smiled a long, slow smile she'd been practicing. It let him know that she realized she was in control of the situation. She asked him if he wanted to check into a hotel somewhere, or maybe he'd stay up in the attic: because she and her new friend planned to be busy in the bedroom for a while.

"Don't overdo it," he told her. "It's possible to injure yourself that way, you know."

"You let me worry about that." She asked for full instructions about the push-button system. She got the doll to rise from the chair and walk up the stairs with her. Edgar went out and got drunk for two days.

She tried out the doll at all the activities he was capable of. She still didn't like him. He didn't look right, he could be uncomfortable without constant monitoring, and his conversation was narrow in the extreme. His sexual prowess was without subtlety, charm, surprise, or even much variety. She didn't believe that her husband had tried to shortchange her; he simply hadn't had the ingenuity to program a better model.

As soon as Edgar sobered up, he knocked at the door. He was full of demands. She didn't listen. She said, "Who was the nerd you modeled this thing on?"

"I didn't. He's a kind of conglomerate."

"Conglomerate certainly isn't as good as whoever it was you picked to make the girl from."

"I didn't pick anyone. Dolly isn't a copy. She's an ideal."

"Oh, my. Well, this one is definitely not my ideal."

"Tough. You made a bargain with me."

"And you gave me a dud."

"I don't believe it."

"He's so boring to talk to, you could go into rigor mortis halfway through a sentence."

"I didn't think you wanted him to be able to discuss the novels of Proust."

"But that could be arranged, couldn't it? You could feed some books into him?"

"Sure."

"And he isn't such a high-stepper in the sack."

"Come on, Helen. Anything more and you'll rupture yourself."

"Reprogramming is what he needs. I can tell you exactly what I want added."

"You can go jump in the lake."

"And I want him to teach me Italian. And flower painting and intermediate *cordon bleu.*"

"No demonstration stuff. I can do a language if you get me the tapes, but they'll have to be changed when you graduate to the next stage. There isn't that much room inside for extra speech."

He was no longer angry or contemptuous. He looked exhausted. He made all the changes she'd asked for on the doll and added a tape of Italian lessons. She tried everything out. The renovated model was a great improvement. She felt worse than ever.

"Where is she?" Edgar pleaded, looking beaten, unhappy, hopeless.

Helen gave him the key to the locker.

Ron stopped taking Dolly to the gym when the boys began to pester him with too many questions. They pressed up around her in a circle, trying to find out what she thought of everything; that got him nervous and mixed her up. And then they started on him. What they most wanted to know was: where did she come from?

He had no answer to that, but no ideas about it, either. Lots of things—some of the most important things in life—remained completely mysterious. That didn't matter. It made more sense just to be happy you had them instead of asking questions about them all the time.

But one day while they were making love, instead of waiting for the end of the cycle she was on, Dolly went into a totally different one. Ron guessed that he must have given her some verbal instruction or physical signal. She started to do things he hadn't realized she knew about. He'd never done them himself, only heard about them. He did his best to keep up. She laughed with pleasure and said, "Does Edgar love his Dolly?"

"Who's Edgar?" he asked.

"Edgar's Dolly's honeybunch, isn't he? Dolly's so happy with her great big gorgeous Edgar, especially with his great big gorgeous—"

"I ain't Edgar," Ron yelled at her. He did something calculated to startle and possibly hurt her. She told him he was wonderful, the best she'd ever had: her very own Edgar.

It wasn't her fault. She didn't know any better. But it just about killed him.

He began to feel jealous. He hadn't wanted to think about how she was made—he'd assumed that she'd been made by machines. But now he had it figured out: she'd been custom-made for one person—a man named Edgar. It still didn't occur to him that this Edgar could have built her himself. He didn't think of things as being made by people. He thought of them as being bought in stores. She would have come from some very fancy place like the big stores where rich people bought diamond necklaces and matching sets of alligator-skin luggage, and so on. You could have all that stuff custom-made.

Someone else had thought her up. She'd been another man's invention. And Ron hadn't been the first to love her; he was sure about that. A sadness began to grow in him. The fact that she couldn't hold a real conversation still didn't bother him, nor that the things she said were always the same. What caused him pain was to hear her calling him by another man's name. He began to think he could live with that too if only in some other phrase she'd occasionally call him by his own name, too.

The sadness began to overshadow his love to such an extent that he thought he'd have to do something about it. He got the suitcase out from the back of the closet and went over the inside. There was a piece of white cardboard tucked into one of the shirt racks in the underside of the top lid. Someone had written a name and address on the card, together with a promise to reward the finder for the return of the case. The name matched the initials on the outside. The first letter of each was E; E for Edgar, maybe. People were so dumb, Ron thought. He'd never put a name or address on anything he was carrying around. Somebody could decide to come after you and clean up.

He put the card in his wallet but he still hadn't really made up his mind.

The next morning everything was decided for him while he was making breakfast in the kitchen. He'd cracked a couple of eggs into the frying pan and was walking over to the garbage pail with the shells. One of them jumped out of his hand. He scooped it up again and threw it out with the others. He meant to wipe a rag over the part of the floor where it had landed but the eggs started to sizzle in the pan. He stepped back to the stove. And at that moment, Dolly came into the room. Before he had a chance to warn her, she was all over the place—skidding and sliding, and landing with a thump.

He picked her up and sat her down on top of the folding stool. He asked, "Are you OK, honey?" She smiled and said she was fine. But he could see, in the middle of her right arm, a dent. He touched the center of the injured place lightly with the tips of his fingers, then he pushed the flat of his hand firmly over the higher edge of the indentation; he hoped that the pressure woud bring the hollow back up to its normal level. But nothing changed. The thing he was afraid of had happened.

"Dolly's hurt," she said. "Dolly needs a four-five-four repair."

"What's that?"

"Dolly needs a four-five-four repair on her arm."

"Uh-huh," he said. He didn't know what to do. All through the day he watched her, to see if the dent got bigger. It didn't; it stayed the same, but at regular intervals she reminded him that she needed to have the arm seen to.

He knew that it was dangerous to keep putting off the moment of action. He should find out what she'd need to have done if something worse went wrong. He could only do that by getting hold of whoever knew how to fix her; and then by trickery, threats, bribes, blackmail or violence, making sure he got the person to help him. If he could find somebody to teach him how to carry out all her repair work himself, that was what he'd like best.

When Edgar began his drive back to the house, Helen was sitting on the living room sofa at the opposite end from the male doll, who was teaching her how to conjugate the verb *to be* in Italian. While she was answering the questions put to her, she stared up at the wall, near the ceiling. She was already tired of him. The renovations had been minimal, she decided. Edgar wasn't able to program a better man, more intelligent, attractive. Perhaps no alterations would make any difference; maybe she just wanted him to be real, even if he was boring. Edgar evidently felt the other way: what he'd loved most about Dolly was that she was perfect, unreal, like a dream. The element of fantasy stimulated him.

For Helen, on the contrary, the excitement was over. Even the erotic thrill was gone. Owning the doll was probably going to be like driving a car—you'd begin by playing with it for fun and thinking it was a marvelous toy: but you'd end up putting it to practical use on chores like the shopping. From now on she'd be using the doll only as a routine measure for alleviating frustration. As soon as Edgar got Dolly back, there'd be plenty of opportunity for feeling frustrated and neglected.

She remembered what Edgar had said about the possible therapeutic value of such a doll. It could be true. There might be lots of people who'd favor the companionship of a nonhuman partner once a week. Or three times a day. No emotions, no strings attached. She thought about her sons: the schoolboy market. There were many categories that came to mind—the recently divorced, the husbands of women who were pregnant or new mothers, the wives of men who were ill, absent, unable, unfaithful, uninterested. And there would be no danger of venereal disease. There were great possibilities. If the idea could be turned into a commercial venture, it might make millions. They could advertise: *Ladies, are you lonely?* She might lend the doll to Gina and see what she thought.

"*Dov'è?*" the doll said.

"*Quì,*" she answered.

The front door opened and banged shut as Edgar's footsteps pounded through the hall. He was running. He burst into the living room and roared, "Where is she? I want the truth this time. And I mean it."

"The doll?" Helen said. "I gave you the key."

"Oh, yes. *But when he got there, the cupboard was bare.* There's nothing inside that locker. It's empty."

"It can't be. It's got two more days to go. Edgar, that was the right key and I put the suitcase in there myself. They aren't allowed to open those lockers before the money runs out. I put in so many—"

"But she isn't there."

"She's got to be. You must have tried the wrong locker. Or maybe the wrong part of the row. All those things look alike."

"I looked everywhere. I saw the right locker. It was

the right one, but there wasn't any suitcase in it. If there was ever anything in it, it's gone now."

"Well, if it's gone," she said, "it's been stolen."

"It can't be stolen. No."

"That's the only explanation I can think of. That's where I put her, so she should still be there. I guess it happens sometimes that they get people forcing the locks, or whatever they do."

"How could you be so careless? To put her in a public place, where anybody could get at her."

"I didn't want to try to hide her in the house. I thought you'd find her."

"But how am I going to get her back?"

"I don't know."

"You'd better know. If I can't find her, Helen—it's the end."

"You could make another one, anytime."

"Impossible." He shook his head slowly and sat down in a chair. He still had his coat on.

Helen said, "I guess we could share Auto."

"Otto?"

"His name," she said, looking at the doll. "Automatico. Auto for short."

"*Buon giorno,*" the doll murmured, making a slight bow from the waist.

Edgar said, "Hi," in a loud, unpleasant tone.

"*Come sta?*" the doll asked.

"That's all right, Auto," Helen said. "You can be quiet now. We've got some things to talk about."

"Bene, signora."

Edgar stared at the doll and snorted. "That's really what you wanted? The guy's a pain in the ass."

"He's getting to be very boring. He's about as interesting as a vibrator."

"I did just what you said."

"But I'm getting sort of sick of him. I always know what's coming next."

"I could program him for random selection—that's the best I can do."

"Maybe what I needed was you."

"It's a little late."

"It was a little late even before you started work on that thing. It began way back, with the computer—didn't it? Remember? When you stopped coming to the table. You'd make me bring in your meals and leave them. You can get a divorce for it nowadays: you cite the computer."

"I could cite Auto here."

"Not if you made him. I don't know what they'd call that—complicity or connivance, or something."

"I think I'll go out for a walk."

"What's your opinion of putting a doll like this on the market? It could become the new executive toy."

"Certainly not."

"Why not? We could make a fortune selling them. You think we should give them away?"

"Why stop with selling? You could run a rental service. Go into the call girl business: charge for every time."

"That's no good. If we didn't agree to sell them, they'd get stolen. People are going to want their own. Would it make a difference to let them out in the world—could somebody copy the way you do them?"

"Not yet. It's my invention. But if there's money in it, you can bet there'd be people after the process. Life wouldn't be worth living. We might not even be safe. That's one of the reasons I decided from the beginning, that if I had any success with the project, I'd keep it to myself."

"You said the dolls could have a therapeutic value."

"Yes, well ... you had me cornered. The therapy was for me. Just as you suspected. I only wanted to make one."

"But all those techniques and materials—the skin, the vocal cords—everything: they could be used in hospitals, couldn't they?"

"No. It's all artificial."

"But it responds to touch and sound. If the dolls can do that, so could separate parts. You could fix almost any physical injury."

"Theoretically."

"It's possible?"

"In theory."

"Then you've got to. I didn't think that far, before. If it's really possible, it's our duty."

"Jesus God, Helen. You take the cake. You just do."

"Me? Who had the idea for this in the first place?"

"Not as a business."

"Oh, I see. That's what makes the difference, is it?"

Out in the hall the phone rang. Helen turned her head, but didn't move. Edgar said, "Aren't you going to get it?"

"I want to finish what we're talking about."

He stood up and went into the hall. She called after him, "Why don't you take your coat off?" He picked up the receiver and barked into it, "Hello?"

A muffled voice came over the wire, saying, "I got something belongs to you."

"Oh?"

"A suitcase."

"Yes," Edgar said quickly. "Where is it?"

"Something was inside it. Something kind of blond, with blue eyes."

"Where is she?"

"I'll do a deal," the voice said. "OK?"

"We can talk about that. Bring her here and we'll discuss it."

"Oh, no. I'm not bringing her anyplace."

"You don't understand. It's a very delicate mechanism. She shouldn't have been away so long. She could be damaged."

"She looks fine."

"She could be damaged and it wouldn't show. Internal injuries. I've got to have a look at her. She's supposed to have regular inspections."

There was silence at the other end. Edgar was covered in sweat. He couldn't think up any more reasons to tell the man why Dolly should come back. He said, "What's your name?"

"Ron," the voice told him.

"Well, Ron, you'd better believe me. If it goes beyond a certain stage, I can't fix anything. I've been worried out of my mind. She's got to come back to the lab."

"Are you the guy that, um ..."

"I'm the designer."

"Uh-huh. OK."

"Now."

"Right. I'll be over." He hung up.

Edgar banged down the phone, threw off his coat and started up the stairs. Helen came out of the living room behind him. "Where are you going?" she said.

"He's got her."

"Who? What have you done with your coat?"

"A man that called up. Ron. He's bringing her over here now."

"Are you going out?"

"Of course not. Dolly's coming here."

"Well, come back and sit down," Helen said. She picked up his coat and hung it in the hall closet.

"I'm the one who knows about her," he muttered. "He can't do anything without me."

Helen pushed him into the living room and sat him down in a chair. She took Auto out, around the corner. She steered him to the downstairs guest room where Edgar's grandmother had once stayed after her leg operation. She stood him up in the closet and closed the door on him.

She waited with Edgar for ten minutes. As soon as they heard the car outside they both ran to the windows.

They saw Ron get out of the car. He was wearing blue jeans and a red T-shirt. Helen said, "Well, he's a bit of a slob, but that's more the kind of thing I had in mind."

"What?"

"To wind up and go to bed with. That man there."

"Mm," Edgar said. He was wondering if he'd be strong enough to tackle a man like that, who looked as if he could knock people down. He began to think about what must have happened all the time Dolly was away. A man like that wouldn't have let her alone, once he'd seen her. Of course not. Edgar was ready to kill him, despite the difference in size.

Ron got Dolly out of the car. He handled her carefully. He walked her up the front steps. He rang the doorbell.

Edgar jerked the door open. The four of them stood looking at each other. Edgar said, "Hello, Dolly."

"Hello there, Edgar-poo," Dolly answered.

"How are you?"

"Dolly's just fine when Edgar's here."

Helen leaned close to Ron. She said, "I'm Helen."

"Ron," he said. "Hi."

"Why don't we all step into the house?" She led the way. She put the three others into the living room, brought in some coffee and sandwiches, and said she'd take Dolly into the next room.

"She stays here," Ron declared.

"She makes me nervous. I'm just going to put her in the guest room. You can come see."

Ron went with her. Helen opened the door to show him the empty room. She smiled at him. "See?" she told him. He laid Dolly down on top of the bed. He looked all around the room and stepped back. Helen closed the door.

Ron followed her back to the living room, where Edgar had changed from coffee to whiskey. Edgar said, "Want a drink?"

Ron nodded. He knew he had the upper hand, drunk or sober. Even over the phone Edgar had sounded like a drip. Maybe he'd put Dolly together, but she was Ron's by right of conquest. Possession was nine-tenths of the law: that was what they said. Let Edgar what's-his-name try to take her back. Ron had a good left as well as a good right: he'd show this Edgar. And the woman was giving him the eye; he might be able to get her to back him up. Now that it occurred to him to notice, he knew who she was, too. She was the woman who'd put the suitcase into the locker.

Edgar began to talk, to plead, to describe the vague glimmerings of the dream he'd had: when Dolly had first come to him as a mere idea. He began to sound so desperate, he'd been so choked up at the sight of Dolly, that Ron pretended to soften. It didn't do any good to scare people too much while you were still trying to line them up; they could go and do something crazy. He said, "Look, Ed, I guess I can see how it is. You feel the same as me. But I can't let her go. You understand? I never thought I'd say it, but we're going to have to do some kind of a deal about sharing."

"Share Dolly? Not for anything."

"That's the way it's got to be. Or—you can make up

your mind to go on without her. I'll just put her in the car and drive her out of your life again. It could be a long time till I needed to bring her back to you. You built her to last, didn't you?"

"I? Yes. I'm the important one. I'm the creator. You two—what are you? I created them."

"You create, maybe," Helen said, "but you don't appreciate."

"That's right," Ron told him. "You couldn't ever love Dolly like I do."

"I invented her, man. She's all mine—she's all me."

Helen said, "If you could hear what you sound like, Edgar."

"I sound like a man who's been treated badly. Helen, you used to understand me."

"Oh? That must have been nice for you. And did you understand me?" She stood up, went to the liquor cabinet and said, "You still haven't brought in the Cinzano. I'll get it." She marched from the room.

Edgar said to Ron, "It's true. You're the one who needs me."

"Right. That's why I'm willing to talk about it. You don't have to bother with this. You can make yourself another one. Can't you?"

"No."

"Sure. You make one, you can make two."

"I made a second one. It was no good."

"What was wrong with her?"

"It was a male replica. For my wife."

"Yeah?"

"It was her price for telling me where she put Dolly."

"No shit. And she didn't like it?"'

"It isn't real enough, apparently. She says she's bored with it."

"Maybe you're only good at them when it's a woman."

"No—I know what the trouble is. It's that I put all my best work, all my ideas and hopes, into that one effort. Dolly was the only time I could do it. I'm like a man who falls in love just once and can't feel the same about any other woman."

Ron didn't believe it. He thought Edgar wouldn't want to give anything to other people: that was the reason why he'd fail.

Edgar made himself a fresh drink. Helen, having found her bottle of vermouth, carried it to the guest room and parked it on the dresser while she took off Dolly's clothes, got Auto out of the closet and then stripped him too. She put him on top of Dolly, arranged both dolls in appropriate positions, and pushed the buttons behind their ears.

She took the bottle into the living room. She poured herself a drink.

Ron said, "OK. I get it. But you've got to see it my way, too. We do a deal, right?"

"I might go back on it," Edgar said.

"And then I'd come after you. And I've got a lot of friends, Ed. They don't all have real good manners, either. You think about that."

Helen drank three large gulps of her drink. She could hear the dolls. After a few seconds, the others heard too.

"What's that?" Edgar said.

"What's going on out there?" Ron asked. "Who else is in this house? You trying to pull something on me?"

"Let's go see," Helen suggested. She bounced toward the door and danced into the hallway. The raucous noise of the dolls drew the two men after her.

She smiled as she flung open the door to show Auto and Dolly engaged on what must have been round two of the full ten-patterned cycle: he whispering, "I could really go for you, you know," and she panting, "Oh, you gorgeous hunk of man," as he began to repeat, "*Bellissima*," with increasingly frenzied enthusiasm.

Edgar and Ron called out curses. They rushed past Helen and grabbed Auto. They tore him away from his exertions. They got him down on the ground and began to kick him. They they hit out at each other. Helen took the opportunity to batter Dolly with the bottle she still held. Vermouth sloshed over the bed, onto the fighting men. Edgar slapped her across the face. The dolls, against all odds, continued to try to fornicate with anything and anyone they encountered, still mouthing expressions of rapturous delight, still whispering endearment and flattery; whereas Helen, Ron and Edgar roared out obscenities: they picked up any weapons they could find, laying about with pokers, shovels, baseball bats. Pieces of the dolls flew across the room. Springs twanged against the walls and ceiling. Reels of tape unwound themselves among the wreckage. And the battle went on; until at last—their faces contorted by hatred—husband, wife and stranger stood bruised, bloody, half-clothed and sweating among the rubble of what they had been fighting over: out of breath in the silent room, unable to speak. There was nothing to say. They stared as if they didn't recognize each other, or the room they were standing in, or any other part of the world which, until just a few moments before, had been theirs.